WALT DISNEY PRODUCTIONS
presents

The Mystery
of the
Missing Peanuts

Random House  New York

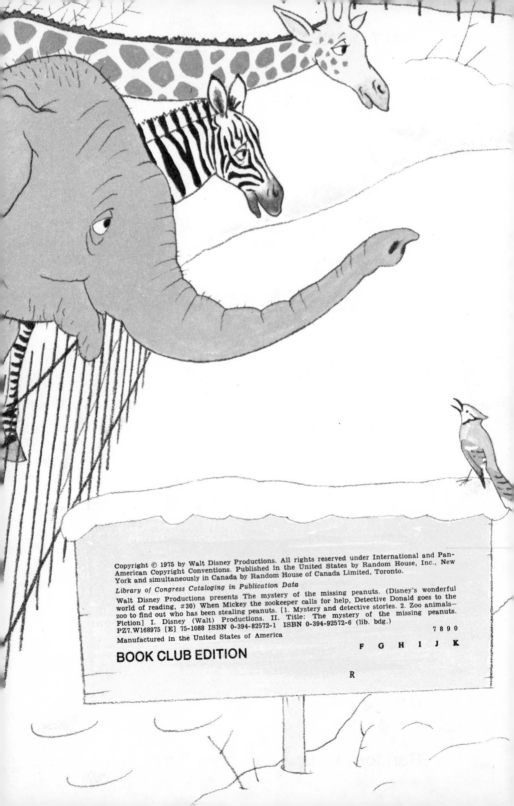

Library of Congress Cataloging in Publication Data
Walt Disney Productions presents The mystery of the missing peanuts. (Disney's wonderful world of reading, #30) When Mickey the zookeeper calls for help, Detective Donald goes to the zoo to find out who has been stealing peanuts. [1. Mystery and detective stories. 2. Zoo animals—Fiction] I. Disney (Walt) Productions. II. Title: The mystery of the missing peanuts.
PZ7.W168975 [E] 75-1088 ISBN 0-394-82572-1 ISBN 0-394-92572-6 (lib. bdg.)   7 8 9 0
Manufactured in the United States of America

BOOK CLUB EDITION

F G H I J K

R

One cold morning Mickey the Zookeeper
was on his way to get breakfast
for the animals.

He hurried to the shed where he kept
the animals' food.

When he reached the shed and unlocked the door,
he saw peanuts all over the floor.

"Oh, no! Not again!" cried Mickey.

Every morning for the past two weeks
the peanut bags had been torn open.

And every morning, more peanuts were missing.

"I have got to catch the thief who is
stealing peanuts," said Mickey.
"I'm going to call Detective Donald!"
He reached for the telephone.

"Mysteries solved," said Detective Donald as he picked up the phone.

"This is the zookeeper," said Mickey. "I need a good detective."

He told Donald about the missing peanuts.

"I'll take the case," said Donald.

Detective Donald threw everything
he might need into his bag.

Then he grabbed his hat and cape
and rushed off to the zoo.

Mickey took Donald
straight to the shed.
"I always keep
the door locked,"
he said.

Donald looked all around.
"Aha!" he cried. "A clue!"
He showed Mickey a hole in the corner.
"Since the door is always locked," said Donald,
"the thief must be getting to the peanuts through
this hole."

He and Mickey ran outside.

There they found another
clue—empty peanut shells.

"I was right about the hole!"
cried Donald. "The thief must have stopped
right here to eat some of the peanuts."

He was hunting for
more clues when— THUMP—
an acorn bounced onto
his head.

When Donald looked up he saw two chipmunks.
"Chip and Dale! Don't bother us!" said Mickey.
"Detective Donald is looking for a thief."

"That sounds like fun," said the chipmunks.
"Let us help."

"I can catch this thief by myself," said Donald.
"I already have a plan."

Donald told Mickey to bring all the animals
to the shed.

He lined them up beside the hole.

"My plan is simple," said Donald.
"I will ask each animal to try to reach
the peanuts through this hole.
The one who can get them
must be the thief."

One by one they tried to reach the peanuts.
But one by one they failed.

Finally there were only three animals left.
The elephant stuck his trunk into the hole.
But he could not reach the peanuts.

The ostrich had a very long neck.
But she could not get her head
through the hole.

The monkey tried
to reach the peanuts
with his long arm.

But his arm was not
long enough.

"That is strange," said Donald.
"Not one of the animals was able
to reach the peanuts."

Just then Chip and Dale jumped
onto the roof of the shed.

"I thought I told you to stay away,"
said Mickey.

"We only want to help," said the chipmunks.

But Detective Donald did not need any help.

He already had another plan to try.

Donald went inside the shed and
unpacked his bag.

He took out a bell, a roll of string,
a hammer, some nails, and a can of paint.

He hammered the nails into the wall
and wound the string around them.

He tied one end of the string to the bell.

He tied the other end around a bag of peanuts.

"That peanut thief will never get past my trap!"
said Donald.

When the trap was set he went outside and
poured blue paint in front of the hole.

Then he climbed into his sleeping bag.

"I'll sleep here tonight," said Donald,
"so I'll be sure to catch the thief."

Late that night the thief came to the shed.
He crept up to the hole.

Quietly he sneaked inside.

Suddenly—C-L-A-A-A-N-G! The bell crashed
to the floor!

The thief had tripped over the string
and rushed out through the hole!

The crash woke up Donald.
"Stop where you are!"
he shouted.
"I have you now!"

He grabbed his bag
and ran after the thief.

The detective was too late.
The thief was gone.
But he had left another clue.
There were footprints in the blue paint.

Donald counted the footprints.
There were eight of them.
"This is the best clue yet!" he cried.
"The thief has eight feet."

Suddenly Chip and Dale appeared.

"What are you looking for now?" they asked.

"Someone with eight legs," said Donald.

Chip and Dale thought for a moment.

"An octopus has eight legs," said Chip.

"That's right!" cried Donald.
He raced off to wake Mickey.

Donald shook Mickey as hard as he could.
He told him about the eight footprints.
"Take me to the octopus," cried Donald.
"Now I know who took the peanuts!"

Together they went into the aquarium.

The octopus was swimming in his tank.

Donald pulled a diving suit out of his bag
and quickly put it on.

Then he took a bag of peanuts
and jumped into the tank.
The octopus swam around and around.
Donald swam right after him.

But no matter how hard
the detective tried, he could not
get the octopus to eat one peanut.

When Donald climbed out he was furious.
"The octopus hates peanuts," he shouted.
"He can't be the thief!"
"Then who can it be?" asked Mickey.

On their way back to the shed, Donald and
Mickey passed two bears splashing in a pool.

"Look, Donald!" cried Mickey. "Those two bears
just made eight footprints. Maybe two animals
made the footprints you found outside the shed.
I think we should be looking for two thieves!"

"And I think I know which two!"
said Donald. "The chipmunks!"
He pulled out his binoculars and
looked into the trees.

He finally found Chip and Dale.

Sure enough—they had blue paint
on their feet.

"There is the thief!" cried Donald.

"Two chipmunks! With four legs each!"

Away he ran to catch them.

When Donald reached the chipmunks' tree, he jumped up and down.

"You are the thief I've been looking for," he cried. "Where are the peanuts you took from the zoo?"

"Peanuts?" cried Chip. "You never told us
you were looking for peanuts!"

"Well, I am," said Donald. "Where are they?"

Chip and Dale led Donald to their underground nest.

"We love peanuts so much," said Chip. "And the zoo has so many."

"We did not think anyone would miss them," said Dale. "We were storing them up for winter."

Donald peeked into the chipmunks' nest.

He saw piles and piles of peanuts.

"They must all go back to Mickey," he said.

Donald brought the peanuts to Mickey.
He brought the chipmunks, too.

"The mystery of the missing peanuts is solved
he said. "I knew I could do it!"

Detective Donald picked up his bag
and said good-by to Mickey.

"If you ever have another mystery,"
he said, "just give me a call."

After Donald had left, Mickey turned to
Chip and Dale.

"You can have peanuts to eat if you
like them so much," said Mickey.
"But from now on you'll have to
work for them."

Mickey gave Chip and Dale a job at the zoo.

Every day they swept up the peanut shells that people threw on the ground.

It was hard work—but it was worth it.

When they were finished, Mickey always gave them all the peanuts they could eat!